★ **BOOK 1** ★
in the **Classroom 13 Series**

Unlucky

THE LOTTERY WINNERS OF **CLASSROOM 13**

By *Honest Lee* & *Matthew J. Gilbert*
Art by **Joelle Dreidemy**

LITTLE, BROWN AND COMPANY
New York • Boston

BIRTHDAY BOOKS FROM COCO
¡FELIZ CUMPLEAÑOS!

Copyright © 2017 by Hachette Book Group, Inc.
CLASSROOM 13 is a trademark of Hachette Book Group, Inc.
Cover and interior art by Joelle Dreidemy.

Cover design by Véronique Sweet. Cover copyright © 2017 by
Hachette Book Group, Inc.

Little, Brown and Company
Hachette Book Group
1290 Avenue of the Americas, New York, NY 10104
Visit us at lb-kids.com

First Edition: June 2017

Little, Brown and Company is a division of Hachette Book Group, Inc.
The Little, Brown name and logo are trademarks of Hachette Book Group, Inc.

The publisher is not responsible for websites (or their content)
that are not owned by the publisher.

Library of Congress Cataloging-in-Publication Data
Names: Lee, Honest, author. | Gilbert, Matthew J. author. | Dreidemy, Joelle, illustrator.
Title: The unlucky lottery winners of Classroom 13 / by Honest Lee and
    Matthew J. Gilbert ; illustrated by Joelle Dreidemy.
Description: First edition. | New York ; Boston : Little, Brown and Company, 2017. |
    Series: Classroom 13 ; 1 | Summary: "Unlucky teacher Ms. Linda LaCrosse wins the
    lottery and shares her winnings with her class. The students fulfill their dreams with
    their newfound wealth, but they soon learn that winning the lottery is not all that
    lucky"— Provided by publisher.
Identifiers: LCCN 2016028103| ISBN 9780316464659 (hardback) |
    ISBN 9780316464642 (e-book) | ISBN 9780316464666 (library edition e-book)
Subjects: | CYAC: Luck—Fiction. | Lotteries—Fiction. | Schools—Fiction. |
    Humorous stories. | BISAC: JUVENILE FICTION / Humorous Stories. |
    JUVENILE FICTION / Social Issues / Friendship. | JUVENILE FICTION /
    Action & Adventure / General. | JUVENILE FICTION / Readers / Chapter Books.
Classification: LCC PZ7.1.L415 Unl 2017 | DDC [Fic]—dc23
LC record available at https://lccn.loc.gov/2016028103

ISBNs: 978-0-316-46465-9 (hardcover), 978-0-316-46462-8 (pbk),
978-0-316-46464-2 (ebook)

Printed in the United States of America

LSC-C

10 9 8 7 6 5 4 3 2 1

 CONTENTS

Chapter 1	Unlucky Ms. Linda	1
Chapter 2	Lucky Ms. Linda	8
Chapter 3	Mason	13
Chapter 4	Emma	18
Chapter 5	William	23
Chapter 6	Sophia	29
Chapter 7	Santiago	33
Chapter 8	Ximena	34
Chapter 9	Jayden Jason	40

Chapter 10	Lily	47
Chapter 11	Jacob	49
Chapter 12	Olivia	56
Chapter 13	Classroom 13	57
Chapter 14	Ava	58
Chapter 15	Teo	61
Chapter 16	Earl	64
Chapter 17	Mark	67
Chapter 18	Mya & Madison	71
Chapter 19	Dev	74
Chapter 20	Ethan	79
Chapter 21	Chloe	84
Chapter 22	Fatima	89

Chapter 23	Yuna	93
Chapter 24	Benji	95
Chapter 25	Preeya	101
Chapter 26	Liam	103
Chapter 27	Isabella	108
Chapter 28	Hugo	110
Chapter 29	Zoey	111
Chapter 30	Really Unlucky Ms. Linda	115

CHAPTER 1
Unlucky Ms. Linda

When *unlucky* schoolteacher Ms. Linda LaCrosse woke up Monday morning, she decided it would be another *unlucky* day. And she was right.

First, she put too much milk on her toast and too much butter in her coffee. Then she forgot her umbrella. It wasn't raining, but she used it to keep birds away. (For some reason, birds liked to swoop down at Ms. Linda and pull out her hair.)

On her way to work, Ms. Linda's car got a flat tire. No one would stop to help. She didn't have a spare tire, she'd left her phone at home, and it started to rain. When she walked to the nearest gas station to ask for help, the cashier was very rude. He snapped, "If you want to use my phone, you have to buy something."

Ms. Linda looked in her purse. All she had was a single dollar bill. "What can I buy for one dollar?"

The cashier pointed to three items. The first was a candy bar. The second was a pine-scented air freshener. And the third was a lottery ticket.

Ms. Linda had a mouth full of cavities, so she passed on the candy bar.

Ms. Linda was very allergic to pine, so she shook her head at the air freshener (after a very violent sneeze).

So Ms. Linda chose the lottery ticket. Being unlucky, she tossed it in her purse without a second thought. She would *not* win. She never won anything.

After Ms. Linda paid for the lottery ticket, the cashier let her use his phone to call a tow truck and a taxi.

When Ms. Linda finally got to her school, she was soaking wet and very late. The principal gave her the evil eye as she rushed down the hall in her heels—*click clack, click clack, click clack*—all the way to her classroom. Her classroom was number 13—which, if you don't know, is a very *un*lucky number.

"Oh, students, I apologize terribly for being terribly late," Ms. Linda said. "I've had quite the terribly—I mean, terri*ble*—morning!"

Of her twenty-seven students, twenty-six of them were present. Santiago Santos was at home with the sniffles. (The poor child was sick more often than not.)

Of the twenty-six students who were in class,

only twenty-four of them were awake. Of those twenty-four, seven were playing video games on their phones. Of the seventeen left, four were gossiping (which is not nice), and three were drawing pictures of butts (which is hilarious).

Of the ten students left, four were playing on the Internet, three were talking about TV shows, two were reading comic books, and one was picking her nose. (She could almost get the booger, but it was just out of reach.)

But of all twenty-seven students, *none* of them were happy that their teacher was here. They were hoping for an entire day of goofing off.

Well, except Olivia. Olivia raised her hand but spoke without waiting to be called on. "Can we start today's lesson already? I'm eager to learn." Olivia was very smart, but she was also very rude.

"Of course, of course!" Ms. Linda said. She pushed her glasses up on her nose and tried to straighten her damp hair (which was a mess because of the birds). "What shall we learn about today? Let's start with current events."

"My dad says the only important news in the world right now is the lottery," said Isabella. She had a horse on her shirt, a horse on her backpack, and a horse barrette in her hair. (Can you tell she liked horses?) "Right now, the lottery is worth *twenty-eight billion dollars!*"

"Oh my!" Ms. Linda said. She wrote *28,000,000,000* on the board. "That is a very big number indeed—after all, it has nine zeroes. Twenty-eight billion dollars is a lot of money. Who would like to do some math?"

"Boo!" some of the students shouted.

"Ce cours est nul!" shouted Hugo, who was from France and spoke only in French.

Ms. Linda remembered her lottery ticket and pulled it out of her purse. "Let's make it fun, then. This morning, I bought a lottery ticket. This lottery ticket cost one dollar. If I win two dollars, what percent is that?"

Only Olivia raised her hand.

"Do you think you'll win?" Ximena asked. "I hear the odds of winning the lottery are *less* likely than the odds of getting struck by lightning."

"I have heard the same thing," Ms. Linda said. "It is *much* more likely that I'll get struck by lightning than win the lottery. After all, I am very *un*lucky."

"If you win, can I have some of the money?" asked Fatima.

"Ooh, me too!" said Jayden Jason James (who other students called Triple J).

All the students wanted some of the lottery money. Ms. Linda shrugged. "I tell you what, class. If I *do* win—which is *very* unlikely—I promise to split my earnings evenly with every single one of you."

All the students in Classroom 13 shouted, "*Really?!*" (Except Hugo. He shouted, "*Sacrebleu!*")

"Of course," Ms. Linda said. "I made a promise, and I must keep my word."

The students hopped up from their desks and huddled together in the middle of the class, whispering among themselves. Finally, they returned to their seats, and Ethan Earhart spoke up. "Ms. Linda? We value your word, but we would feel much more comfortable with your promise if we could get it in writing. Would you mind signing a contract and pinkie-swearing to share the money if you win?"

Ms. Linda thought creating a contract was a good lesson for the class. So together, they drew up a contract, which Ms. Linda and every student signed. Then, one by one, every student in Ms. Linda's class walked to the front of the room and did a pinkie swear with Ms. Linda. For the rest of the day, the students were nicer than usual. Perhaps Ms. Linda's luck was changing.

That day after school, as Ms. Linda walked home, she was struck by lightning—twice.

CHAPTER 2
Lucky Ms. Linda

When schoolteacher Ms. Linda LaCrosse woke up on Tuesday morning, she was in the hospital. She had survived both lightning strikes, and everyone kept saying, "You are *very* lucky!"

On Wednesday, when Ms. Linda LaCrosse woke up in her own home, she decided it would be a very *lucky* day for a change.

And she was right.

First, she put the right amount of milk into her coffee and the right amount of butter on her toast. Then she turned on her TV and saw the winning numbers for the lottery.

Ms. Linda LaCrosse had won.

When Ms. Linda received her winnings, she did exactly as she said she would and split the winnings with her students.

"Are you serious?!" asked Preeya.

"I am very serious," said Ms. Linda LaCrosse.

"But why don't you just take the money and run?!" asked Liam. "That's what *I* would do."

"Well, then it's a good thing that *I* won and you did not," said their teacher. She wore nice new clothes and had fancy laser eye surgery, so no more contacts. Her hair also looked very nice. Now that she had a limo and a chauffeur, the birds never had the chance to pester her.

"Are you really going to give us equal shares of the money?" asked William (who didn't trust anybody).

"Of course," said Ms. Linda. "A promise is a promise. What kind of teacher would I be if I didn't keep my word?"

In this lottery, Ms. Linda was the *only* winner—which meant she now had $28,000,000,000 in her bank account. "Twenty-eight billion dollars divided by one teacher and twenty-seven students equals one billion dollars each—"

"Hold on!" shouted Ethan. He held up the contract. "You only made a promise to the students who were *in* class that day! Santiago Santos was home sick."

"Yeah!" the students shouted.

"Wait, what?" said Santiago with a sniffle. (He was still sick.)

"But Santiago is part of our class," said Ms. Linda, "even if he was home sick that day." Ms. Linda wanted to be fair.

"Nope! No way! Nuh-uh," the other students disagreed.

"Think of the Constitution of the United States and the Declaration of Independence," said Ethan Earhart. He was a gifted speaker and a natural-born leader. "George Washington and Benjamin Franklin signed the Constitution. Santiago did not."

"That is true," Ms. Linda agreed.

"Thomas Jefferson and John Hancock signed the Declaration of Independence," Ethan continued. "Santiago did not."

"That is also true," Ms. Linda agreed again.

"And only the students who were *in* class that day *signed* this contract. Santiago was *not* and did *not*."

"That is also true," Ms. Linda was forced to agree.

"Then I present a question before the courts," Ethan said, as if talking to an invisible judge. "Would it be fair for Santiago Santos to take

money for a contract he did *not* sign? *We* have a right to that money, but *he* does not!"

All the students—except Santiago, who was wiping a rather runny nose—clapped and cheered.

Ultimately, Ms. Linda had to agree. "I am sorry, Santiago Santos. But you *were* sick that day. And we *did* sign a contract. I'm afraid you will *not* get an equal share of my lottery winnings."

For the next hour, Ms. Linda wrote a check to every student in her class—with one obvious (sniffling) exception.

Later that day, *twenty-five* students walked out of class with a check for over a billion dollars: $1,037,037,037.04 each, to be exact.

(You probably think I've made a mistake. But I haven't. Trust me. My name is Honest Lee.)

The next day, no one showed up to class except for Santiago Santos. He was still sick, but he vowed to never miss a day of school again.

CHAPTER 3
Mason

Mason was not the smartest kid in Classroom 13. He was not the most handsome (that honor went to Mark, of course). And he was not the funniest. But, man, could he play sports.

He was a natural-born athlete but loved soccer the most. He was the county's record holder for most goals in a single soccer game.

So, naturally, the first (and only) thing the

school's star soccer player bought with his $1,037,037,037.04 was a cow.

(Like I said, he was *not* the smartest kid in Classroom 13.)

✮ ✮ ✮

Mason had been walking home from school with his check, when he met a farmer.

"Why the long face, son?" the farmer asked.

"Today I got a check for over a billion dollars, and I'm not sure what to spend it on."

"Well, that's easy," said the farmer, with sly eyes. "Buy a cow."

"A cow?" Mason asked.

"Of course! Cows are an investment. I have dozens of cows. Each one is worth millions. But this one right here? Daisy is special. She's worth well over a billion dollars. Heck, maybe even more! She's a friend for life. She can provide love and warmth all her days—not to mention all the milk you could drink! Add a little chocolate syrup, and *boom*! Ya got chocolate milk! Daisy here is priceless!"

Mason *did* like chocolate milk.

So he gave the farmer his check and took Daisy home.

Mason changed Daisy's name to Touchdown. That way, anytime he called for her, she reminded him of scoring a goal in soccer. (Which was incorrect, since a touchdown was a goal in football. Like I said, Mason? *Not* the smartest.)

But the sly farmer was right about one thing: They were instant friends.

Mason and Touchdown played soccer together (though Touchdown didn't kick the ball so much as just *moo*). They watched Netflix together (though Touchdown didn't watch so much as just *moo*). And they walked to school each morning (during which time Touchdown stopped to eat grass and would occasionally— you guessed it—just *moo*).

Touchdown provided Mason with fresh milk every morning, and Mason cleaned up the big piles of poop that Touchdown left in his front yard.

The pair were inseparable. The perfect team.

"I love you, Touchdown," Mason said.

"Moooooo," Touchdown *moo*ed.

The soccer champ and the cow spent all day together, except at school. Even though they walked together, Ms. Linda wouldn't let Touchdown in the classroom. "Classroom 13 already has a class pet," Ms. Linda said. "Touchdown might make Earl the Hamster jealous. It's best that Touchdown wait outside."

Mason honored Ms. Linda's wishes. He left Touchdown to roam freely, nap under the playground slide, and graze on the soccer field all day. Before long, this turned into quite the problem.

Within a month, there was no more grass on the field—Touchdown had eaten it all. Instead of a soccer field, there was just a giant mud pit. To make matters worse, the other soccer players kept complaining that their cleats were covered in "cow pies." Mason didn't understand the uproar—pie was a good thing, wasn't it?

The school's athletic department demanded someone pay for the damages.

Not having any money left, Mason didn't know what to do. Luckily, Touchdown did. Touchdown took a day job as the school crossing guard. Nothing stops traffic quite like a cow in the middle of the road.

CHAPTER 4
Emma

When Emma Embry was a little girl, she begged her parents for one thing—a cat. She didn't care if it was a Manx cat with no tail or an alley cat with one eye, all she wanted was a cat. (She was so desperate, she would have been happy with one of those scary-looking *hairless* cats.)

But Mr. and Mrs. Embry were "interior decorators"—which is just a fancy way of saying "people who get paid to tell you what furniture to buy." And, yes, people paid Mr. and Mrs. Embry money (and lots of it) to tell them what kind of furniture to buy.

Because of their job, Mr. and Mrs. Embry were expected to have a perfect home. They had fancy furniture with long fancy names, like "Renaissance armoires" and "Louis XVI Baroque chairs." They had silk drapes and velvet carpet. Everything in their home was expensive or priceless or one of a kind.

That meant they would have absolutely *no* animals in the house that might pee or poo or vomit on their precious interior decorations. Thus, no cat for Emma.

Unfortunately for Mr. and Mrs. Embry, Emma came home one day with a check for $1,037,037,037.04. And she planned to spend every dime of it on what she'd always wanted: *cats*.

The next day, Emma bought every cat in the state—whether it was from a store or from an alley. She had them all shipped directly to her house. Within twenty-four hours, Mr. and Mrs. Embry's dream house became their *nightmare* house.

Curtains were shredded, couches were covered in hair, and anything that looked like a bird (or had a bird on it) was utterly destroyed.

"Our beautiful home!" Emma's parents cried. "What have you done, you terrible child?"

"For years, your home was more important to you than me," Emma said. "Now, my dream *pet* has ruined your dream *house*. Fair is fair."

Mr. and Mrs. Embry growled and screamed and threw a tantrum. When they were done, they told Emma, "If you have so much money, perhaps you and your cats should go live somewhere else."

"That's a fantastic idea!" Emma said. She'd always wanted to live on an island of cats.

Emma bought a large island in the Pacific Ocean off the coast of Polynesia. She renamed it Cats Island. (Not to be confused with Tashirojima, Japan—also known as Cat Island.)

Then she chartered a plane to take her and all her cats to their new home. She built a castle full of pillows and scratching posts. The televisions only played movies and shows about cats. Outside, there was a massive garden of catnip.

There was only one law on Cats Island:

NO DOGS ALLOWED.

Emma started a stray adoption service so that anytime a cat needed a home, it was flown (first class, of course) to Cats Island.

Emma finally had everything she ever dreamed of. There was only one problem—it turns out Emma is *severely allergic to cats*.

Her eyes swelled up, then sealed shut with icky-sticky eye goo. She broke out in hives, and

her whole body became itchy. She couldn't stop scratching. But the worst part was the sneezing. Every thirty seconds, she sneezed a terrible and loud and snotty sneeze that scared all the cats away. And no matter how many allergy medicines she took, she was still allergic to her favorite thing in the world—cats.

Eventually, she had to leave Cats Island and go home.

CHAPTER 5
William

All the students in Classroom 13 were careful not to use the p-word around William. You know the one—*paranoid*.

"I'm not paranoid!" William yelled. "It's not paranoia if someone's *really* after you. I'm telling you, we're all being watched. *That* woman has been watching me *all day!*"

"But, William," Ms. Linda said, "I'm your

teacher. I'm *supposed* to be watching you. That's how school works."

"Aha!" he shouted back. "So you admit you've been spying on me! It's a conspiracy!" He looked at the others with a smirk on his face. "Told you."

The other students were used to William being the most ~~paranoid~~ suspicious kid in Classroom 13. So, when William decided his life was in danger because of his lottery money, they shrugged it off.

"But, you guys," he said, "someone is going to try to rob me. Or worse! I just know it."

"Then hire bodyguards," Ethan told him. "Of course, if you don't pay them enough, they could turn on you, too."

William agreed. *Trust no one.*

He left school that day, taking a different path home than he normally did—in case he was being followed. He changed clothes as he snuck through the park, trying different disguises he had in his backpack: a neck brace, a nun's habit, a cowboy hat with a mustache. He finally decided to dress like an old man.

He folded up the lottery check and hid it in his shoe. He changed his outfit, stuffed his clothes with newspaper, then added an oversized scarf and a hat. "No one will recognize me now," he muttered.

Out of the corner of his eye, William thought he saw an unmarked car pursuing him with bad guys inside. He hopped on a bus going the opposite way from his house. It took him clear across town. *This will throw them off my trail,* he thought.

"You look just like my grandfather," said a young woman on the bus. "Please, take my seat." So William sat down. But then the woman started staring at him. He was sure that she wanted to steal his billion-dollar check too.

At the next stoplight, he ran off the bus.

When William got home, he ditched the disguise. But with each passing minute, he grew more worried. He was certain he would be robbed at any second.

He cut a hole in his mattress to stuff the check inside. But he became ~~paranoid~~ scared that the check would get stuck in the mattress springs and he'd have to rip it out. (Last he checked, the bank wouldn't accept paper shreds.)

He needed a new plan. But where would his check be safe?

William jumped when his bedroom door opened. It was his parents.

"Son?" his dad said. "Is everything okay?"

"Someone's trying to steal my money!"

"Don't be para—I mean, silly," his mom said. "Why would someone steal your allowance?"

"Not that money. *This* money." William showed them his lottery check.

"Oh!" his dad said.

"Why don't *we* hide it for you?" his mom said. "If someone is after you, no one will suspect we have it."

"And as adults, we know lots of great hiding spots," his dad added.

"Great idea!" William said. "Take that, bad guys!" He hugged his parents, thanked them, and went to sleep. (Being ~~paranoid~~ cautious all day was exhausting.)

The next morning, William peeked out his windows. No one was spying on him. His parents' plan had worked.

As he went to thank his parents, he found they weren't home. His parents' clothes were gone. So were their suitcases. And so was his pet goldfish, Goldie. "That's weird," he whispered.

William's mind started to wonder. Had his mom and dad stolen his money? Would they really run off without saying good-bye? Were

they thousands of miles away on a beach some-where, sipping umbrella drinks and laughing about their double cross? And was the goldfish—that shifty-eyed sneak—secretly the mastermind of the whole thing? And was Goldie even his goldfish's real name?!

William chuckled to himself. *That all sounds so...so...~~stupid~~ paranoid*, he thought.

Soon, William would learn that his paranoia was correct. His parents *had* run off with his money—and they were *not* coming home.

CHAPTER 6
Sophia

When she was born, Sophia was partially deaf. Now she wore hearing aids so she could hear. And every night, as she drifted off to sleep, she listened to "Sounds of the Rain Forest" on her laptop. (She found the exotic sounds of insects and birds and monkeys quite soothing.)

You see, Sophia loved nature. She talked to plants for hours, protected bugs, and hugged trees. (Sometimes they were rather long, *awkward* hugs.)

Because of that, Sophia believed the term "tree hugger" was invented for her. Per copyright law, she thought she deserved a nickel every time someone said it. Not that she needed any nickels. Now she was a billionaire.

After cashing her check for $1,037,037,037.04, she flew to South America and bought the Amazon. Not a piece of the Amazon—the *whole* Amazon rain forest.

Then she put up handmade signs all around it that read: NO SAWS ALLOWED!, PROTECTED AREA—KEEP OUT CONSTRUCTION JERKS!, and TREES ARE FOR HUGGING—NOT FOR CUTTING! (The signs were made on recycled paper, of course.)

She put up hundreds of these signs without using a single drop of bug spray to protect herself. After all, she believed that bug spray harmed the atmosphere and hurt innocent bugs.

But the Amazon insects didn't care about Sophia the way she cared about them. Sophia was bitten by twenty different species of bugs during her travels. By the time she was done, her skin was swollen with hives, warts, and awful rashes.

Next, she built protective sanctuaries for all the endangered species there. She paid local hunters to stay away and spread the word that the Amazon was "under new management."

"Whatever you say," the hunters said, shivering in their boots. Sophia's face was so monstrous from all the bug bites, she looked like a monster from a horror movie.

Sophia didn't care what she looked like. If the pygmy marmosets could talk, she knew they'd thank her. (Instead, most of them flung poop at her.)

Before she could buy Madagascar and save its rain forest, Sophia ran out of money. Property taxes, land deals, flights, bribes, and sign-making supplies were not cheap. The fat black markers alone were five bucks each.

Still, Sophia had saved the rain forest.

"I love nature, I love nature," Sophia repeated to herself over and over while she itched and itched and itched....

CHAPTER 7
Santiago

Santiago didn't get a dime from Ms. Linda's lottery winnings. That's what happens when you stay home sick.

CHAPTER 8
Ximena

Every day, on Ximena Xuxa's walk home from school, she stopped at the strip mall. She would high-five the florist, pick up some *caramelos* for her *abuela* (that's Spanish for "grandma"), and grab a new brochure at the travel agency.

(Her family couldn't afford to travel, but Ximena liked getting lost in the pictures of faraway islands and famous landmarks.)

But not today.

Today, with her check for $1,037,037,037.04, Ximena ran home as fast as she could. She skipped her usual stop at the strip mall.

The florist was ready to high-five her, but all he saw was a girl-shaped blur run by. His hand was raised but left high-five*less* in the air.

The owner of the sweets shop looked at her clock. She wondered if Ximena was sick. She always picked up *caramelos* for her *abuela*. But not today.

Even the travel agent—who let Ximena take all the travel brochures she wanted (free of charge)—was worried. The new Grand Canyon brochures weren't going to look at themselves.

At that moment, on the other side of the tracks, in the poor side of town, Ximena bolted through her front door like an Olympic runner.

"Mamá...Papá...Abuela..." Ximena said, out

of breath. She held up her check. "You're not going to believe this...."

And they didn't.

You see, the Xuxa family had very little money. Mr. and Mrs. Xuxa both worked two jobs and worked hard for every dollar. So they found it hard to believe their daughter could become an instant billionaire simply by showing up to school.

"You're right. I don't believe it!" Mr. Xuxa said. He stared at the check.

"Me neither!" her mom said. She kept counting the commas.

"Truly, *mija?!*" her *abuela* said from her bed. "I am so happy for you, *mija*. Now you can see the world, just like you've always wanted."

"Will you come with me, Abuela?" Ximena asked.

"I wish I could, but no. I am too old and too tired. But you should go."

Abuela was Ximena's best friend. She didn't want to see the world without her. But as Ximena stared at her collected travel brochures, she had an idea. If she couldn't take her *abuela* to see the world, then she would bring the world to her *abuela*.

✱   ✱   ✱

First, Ximena *rented* the Statue of Liberty. She had it airlifted from Liberty Island right to her driveway. Ximena thought it was much *less* green in person than in the brochures. Ximena repainted the statue electric pink and gave her a pair of bright yellow sunglasses. (When she was returned to New York City, everyone seemed to like the new look.)

Ximena then rented Mount Rushmore. It was airlifted from South Dakota to her backyard. She agreed with the brochure that the monument was "impressive," but she thought it needed something extra. So she hired a sculptor to chisel her *abuela*'s face next to President Lincoln's. It was her *abuela*'s idea to add a mustache and a Mohawk.

Ximena called the French government about renting the Eiffel Tower, but someone had already bought it. (Ximena wondered if it was someone in her class.)

Ximena spent her fortune renting other famous landmarks. She rented the Great Sphinx from Egypt, the Great Wall of China from China, the Taj Mahal from India, and the Leaning Tower of Pisa from Italy. She even rented Big Ben from England. (Though it was only temporary, the queen was *not* pleased about it.)

Abuela loved everything that Ximena brought home for her to see—except for Stonehenge, which Abuela called "just a bunch of rocks."

When she ran out of enough money to rent new landmarks, Ximena had just enough left over to buy her *abuela* a brand-new (and very comfy) bed and a lifetime supply of *caramelos*.

Together, they looked at new travel brochures. They didn't have a lot of money, but they had a lot of love—which, like the brochures, was free of charge.

CHAPTER 9
Jayden Jason

Jayden Jason James (or Triple J, as some called him) was the most popular kid in the entire school. He had a standing invitation to sit at any table in the cafeteria. He was voted class president four times in a row (in the same election). And he was always the first to be asked to study groups, sleepovers, and birthday parties.

He was the closest thing to a celebrity Classroom 13 had.

But he never let fame go to his head. Triple J was a people pleaser and a genuinely nice person. If he missed someone's event, he felt terrible.

And since he was always asked to attend everything (and there was only *one* of him to go around), Triple J was exhausted all the time. He needed a break.

So with his lottery winnings, he decided to *clone* himself.

He held a press conference about it on the playground. Ava acted as his press secretary and pointed to kids in the crowd (one at a time) to ask questions.

"How many clones will there be?" Teo asked.

"With the new clones, there'll be enough of me to go around," Triple J said. "In the past, I know I've disappointed some of you because my schedule was overbooked. Soon that will be a thing of the past. I hate missing events!"

Hands shot up again. Ava pointed to Dev, who asked, "What do we call your clones? Will they have different names? And if so, can I name one?"

"No different names," Triple J said. "That's too confusing. We're numbering them. I'll be J-1, and the first clone will be J-2, and then J-3, and so on."

"We have time for one more question," Ava said.

Chloe shouted, "Cloning is *not* ethically or morally sound!"

"That's not a question," Ava said. "Looks like that's all the time we have for today. No further questions, thank you."

✮   ✮   ✮

Triple J hired the world's most brilliant scientists to clone him.

"That is immoral!" one scientist said.

"It's dangerous!" said another.

"How will you know who you are?!" said a third.

Triple J handed them his money. The scientists suddenly changed their minds and got to work.

The procedure was a success. Within days, there were four brand-new perfect clones of Triple J. (You might think four isn't very many, but clones are quite expensive. You could buy a space station for far less money.)

Triple J put a plan together: J-2 would attend all academic events like study sessions, quiz bowls, mathlete meetings, and school play try-outs. J-3 would handle all the athletic stuff like baseball, basketball, soccer, and (of course) bob-sledding. J-4 would take care of all family responsibilities like birthdays, Sunday dinners, and movie nights. And J-5 (the fourth and final clone) would appear at all social gatherings like sleepovers, pizza parties, and recess.

Triple J would never miss a single thing again. (At least that was the plan.)

For one perfect week, the Triple J clones were everywhere at once. J-5 attended game nights at Fatima's while J-3 was bobsledding with Mason. At the same time, J-2 was studying with Sophia and Teo for their history test, just as J-4 was settling in to watch movies with his family for movie night.

Of course, the original Triple J (J-1) wasn't at any of these events. People began to complain. They didn't want a clone. They wanted the famous original Jayden Jason James. They wanted the real deal. Triple J was frustrated, but he wanted everyone to be happy.

Triple J decided to go back to the way things were before. He would be tired, but at least everyone would be happy.

Triple J held a press conference about it on

the playground. Teo acted as his press secretary and pointed to kids in the crowd (one at a time) to ask questions.

"Why are you giving up on your clone plan?" Ava asked.

"I want everyone to be happy," Triple J said.

Hands shot up again. Teo pointed to Dev, who asked, "What happened to your clones?"

"I sent them to live on a farm," Triple J said. "But instead, they ran away and joined the circus. Don't worry. They are all very happy."

"We have time for one more question," Teo said.

Chloe shouted, "*I told you*—cloning is *not* ethically or morally sound!"

"That's not a question," Teo said. "Looks like that's all the time we have for today. No further questions, thank you."

✷   ✷   ✷

After that, the original, famous Triple J was back. Everyone was happy to have the *real* Triple J—not some secondhand clone.

Then again, how would they know the difference? Clones are the exact same in every way. They look the same, they talk the same, they even fart the same.

What if the *real* Triple J was the one that ran away to the circus?

Strangely enough, some of the students of Classroom 13 have wondered the exact same thing. I've told them just to ask Triple J the next time they see him...

On the basketball court...

Or at the spelling bee...

Or in the kitchen making popcorn for family movie night...

Or at the mall with friends...

Or...

Hey! Wait a second!

CHAPTER 10
Lily

Lily is a girl of few words. For instance, if you asked her how her weekend was, she would likely grunt, "Fine." Or, "Cool." Or, "Meh."

And if you asked her what she wanted to be when she grew up, she'd answer, "Astronaut." She wanted to go into space and explore the stars.

According to her dad, her first spoken word

was "NASA." He thought it was rather cute—because he thought baby Lily was mispronouncing "Dada." But no, she really *was* saying "NASA."

When Ms. Linda informed the class they were going to become billionaires, the other students talked a mile a minute about stuff they were going to purchase or things they were going to do. Lily only looked at her check and said, "NASA."

So Lily bought NASA. Yes, the National Aeronautics and Space Administration is now owned by Lily Lin from Classroom 13.

Lily's been tight-lipped (no surprise there) about the new rocket she has them building for her. I've heard construction will be finished in about twenty years. But if you ask Lily when it'll be ready for blastoff, she just says, "Soon."

CHAPTER 11
Jacob

Jacob Jones knew exactly what he was going to buy with his winnings. (Or more accurately, *who* he was going to buy.) He announced, "I'm going to buy a family!"

This confused the other students of Classroom 13.

"But you already have one of those," Benji said.

It was true. Jacob *did* have a family—but he didn't like them. He had a mother and a father who both kept to themselves. They never hugged Jacob, or spent time with him, or asked how his day was. Instead, when they came home from work, Mr. and Mrs. Jones would retire to their separate bedrooms.

To keep him company, Jacob left the TV on twenty-four hours a day.

There were lots of shows he liked, but there was one show he *loved*. It was called *Just the Twenty-Two of Us*. It was a classic comedy about the Jordans—a quirky family of twenty-two people crammed together in the same small house. If that wasn't hilarious enough, Mr. Jordan, the dad, was a basketball coach who treated his family like a team. When things got too crazy at home, he'd blow his whistle and shout, "Time-out! Family foul!"

Then everyone would laugh—the family, the

live studio audience, and, of course, Jacob. Jacob loved the catchphrases. *"Time-out!"* he'd repeat, blowing an imaginary whistle. *"Family foul!"*

(Jacob liked to pretend the studio audience was laughing at his jokes, too.)

Jacob loved Coach Jordan's family more than anything. They were always there for one another. And they were always there for him. He wanted to be one of the Jordans. But that wasn't going to happen. That would take a miracle...

...or $1,037,037,037.04 in cash.

✷　　✷　　✷

The minute the check cleared, Jacob kicked his parents out of the house and moved all the Jordans in.

"Good-bye, Jacob Jones!" he said to himself. "Hello, Jacob *JORDAN!*"

Jacob was so excited, he greeted his new

family at the door by singing the *Just the Twenty-Two of Us* theme song:

> *"Having a family's like having a team,*
> *Twenty-two people LIVING THE DREAM!*
> *Our family's got game,*
> *Our family's got trust,*
> *So let's work together,*
> *Just the twenty-two of us!"*

When he finished the song, Jacob bowed. He expected his new family would cheer and clap and surround him with a group hug—just like they did on the show.

But they didn't.

In fact, not one member of the cast looked happy. Instead, Jacob's new sitcom family began asking him some very *un*-sitcom questions.

"Is this *not* catered?" Jeremy Jordan (the youngest family member) asked.

"How long is this gonna take? I have a photo

shoot at nine and another thing at ten," Jess Jordan (the older sister) said.

"What's the Wi-Fi password here? I need to watch my horse races," Jordan Senior (the grandpa) said, blowing cigar smoke everywhere.

"What's my motivation for this scene?" Coach Jordan asked Jacob. "Am I like, *'Family foul,'* or am I more like, *'Family FOULLLLLL'*?!"

Over the next few days, things got worse. His new family didn't want to sing their theme song. (Instead they complained a lot.) They didn't want to get into hilarious situations at the grocery store. (They didn't want to clean up after themselves either.) They didn't want to laugh over a family recipe gone wrong. (But they did expect five-star chefs to prepare all their meals.) They didn't even care if Jacob applauded when they entered a room. (In fact, they gave him strange looks when he did.)

Jacob didn't understand why everyone was

acting so weird. They weren't acting like the TV characters he loved. They were acting like...like... *actors*.

Hoping they would come around, Jacob gave them *more* money to act like his favorite characters. But they moaned and groaned the whole time. At the end of each day, their agents called and asked for more money.

And the catchphrases? They charged Jacob *extra* every time they said them.

Jacob was broke by the end of the first week.

Finally, he had enough. He blew his whistle. *"Time-out! Family foul!"* he shouted. "None of you are acting like how you are on TV! Don't you understand? The people you portray on TV are wonderful. They bring laughter to the world. Don't you want to be better in real life?"

The actors shrugged. Janice (the mother) asked, "Does it pay more?"

"Actually, I'm out of money," Jacob said.

Jacob expected an *"Awwwwwwww!"* from the studio audience.

But there wasn't one.

The mob of snobby TV stars stomped out of his house and back into their limousines without a word.

Coach Jordan didn't even let Jacob keep the whistle.

Jacob didn't want to be Jacob Jordan anymore. He wanted to be Jacob *Jones* again.

So he sold his TV, got enough money to move his real parents back home, and swore off TV for the rest of his life.

Then he went and got himself a *free* library card.

CHAPTER 12
Olivia

More than anything, Olivia loved to learn. Even though she was still young, she wanted to stay in college as long as she could when she was older. So rather than spend any of her money, she put it all in the bank.

Why would she do such a thing?

Because college is very expensive. (Just ask your parents.)

CHAPTER 13
Classroom 13

Like Santiago, Classroom 13 didn't get a dime either—even though it *was* there on the day Ms. Linda promised to share her winnings. The Classroom wasn't a student, but it had feelings, too—and its feelings were hurt.

The 13th Classroom vowed revenge on all the students one day....

CHAPTER 14
Ava

Ava was so excited when she got home with her check for $1,037,037,037.04, she asked her parents right away if she could start spending the money. They said, "No."

She spent it anyway.

If you know Ava, you know that she is a great friend. When William forgot his lunch one day, Ava shared her lunch with him. When Chloe spilled cranberry juice on her blouse before class photos, Ava lent her a sweater. And when Lily told her a secret, Ava promised not to tell anyone—and she didn't.

Ava wanted to share her newfound wealth with her friends. So she texted everyone and asked what she should spend the money on. The next day, she did exactly what would make her friends happy.

She bought an island—a *whole* island—in Hawaii. (Not one of the big ones, but one of the small ones.)

Ava built a huge castle on the island. The castle had everything her friends could think of: Tennis courts. Swimming pools. A movie theater. A dock with boats and Jet Skis. A ranch full of horses. It even had a waterslide park and cotton-candy machines.

She and her friends couldn't wait until it was ready. It took a while to build everything they

wanted. But once it was done, Ava rented a private plane and flew everyone there.

For forty-seven hours, they had the most amazing time.

Then the ground started to shake. Puffs of black smoke began to burp out of the island mountain. The island's "director of fun" (who was actually Ava's mom, Heather) called Ava and said, "Hi, sweetie. I think maybe we should leave."

At first, Ava refused. But when the volcano erupted, she decided her mom was right. She and her friends (and all the horses) crammed onto her private jet and took off into the sky.

As they flew to safety, Ava looked out the window and watched her island sink beneath the surface of the ocean. "Oh well," she said. "At least now the fish have a cool place to hang out."

CHAPTER 15
Teo

Teo loved roller coasters, junk food, and fireworks. (He also loved dogs.) So when he got his check for $1,037,037,037.04, he wasn't sure how he was going to spend it. At least not until he realized that there was a certain amusement park that has roller coasters and junk food and daily fireworks shows.

Teo didn't even bother asking his parents if he could spend the money. He just started spending.

He called up the owners of this amusement park franchise and asked if he could buy it. They thought it was a prank call and hung up.

Teo called back. He asked again. They said, "No," then hung up.

Teo called back a third time and explained, "I have 1.037 billion dollars, and I would like to buy your amusement park."

"Oh! That's a lot of money. In that case, you can buy *one* of our theme parks."

"There's more than one?!" he asked.

"Of course!"

Teo ended up buying the one in Florida. He invited all his friends and cousins and uncles and aunts and grandparents for a week. (Even though he didn't want to, he finally told his parents they could come, too.)

For forty-seven hours, they rode roller coasters and ate too much junk food. Then ate more junk food and rode more roller coasters, until everyone had thrown up at least once on one of the rides. Except his dad, Luis, who had thrown up several times.

Teo, his friends, and his family didn't have to wait in any lines and all the food was free. (Well, it wasn't totally free. They still had to tip the waitstaff.) It was a truly amazing time. But the best part hadn't even happened yet. Teo was saving the best part for last—the fireworks show.

At the end of the second day, Teo demanded that the theme park have the biggest, brightest fireworks show they'd ever had in the history of fireworks shows. And they did. It turned out to be too much.

The world-famous amusement park burned down.

Teo was super annoyed for several days. Then he remembered he still had some money left: $37,037.04, to be exact. So he bought a German shepherd, a Siberian husky, and a new Xbox, and then took his family on a cruise. It was a really nice vacation.

CHAPTER 16
Earl

Remember how you thought I made a mistake on page 12? Well, I didn't.

The teacher (Ms. Linda) won $28 billion—that is, $28,000,000,000.

She agreed to *split it evenly* with each of her students (27 in total), minus one (Santiago, who was sick that day). That means 26 students.

If you add Ms. Linda, that's 27 people total.

So $28,000,000,000 divided by 27 is $1,037,037,037.04.

At the end of Chapter 2, I said: "Later that day, *twenty-five* students walked out of class with a check for over a billion dollars: $1,037,037,037.04 each, to be exact."

(Go on. Flip back to page 12 and check. See? I'm telling the truth. I'm Honest Lee.)

Did you notice? There were twenty-*six* students who won the lottery in the class, but only twenty-*five* students left that day. Why is that?

Simple. One of the "students" never left. You see, Earl lives in the classroom. Earl is a hamster.

✳   ✳   ✳

During the first week of school, Ms. Linda counted her students. She had twenty-six in total. But all the kids insisted that the class pet, Earl the Hamster, was also a student.

Ms. Linda did not like arguing with her students, so she agreed. Earl became a student of Classroom 13 that day.

But how did Earl get the money? Well, he signed the contract, of course.

You see, Liam was something of a prankster—meaning he loved to pull pranks. And when he signed the contract for the lottery winnings, he thought he'd be funny and have Earl sign it, too. He colored the hamster's paw with a black marker and stamped it on the contract.

When it came time for everyone to collect their winnings, Liam explained it to Ms. Linda. "Well, if Earl signed the contract, then he's entitled to his share, too. After all, I am a woman of my word," she said.

So, yes, Earl received a check for $1,037,037,037.04.

What did he do with it? He shred it up with his cute little claws. Then he peed on it.

CHAPTER 17
Mark

Mark was the most handsome student in Classroom 13, and all the girls had a crush on him. But he only had eyes for one woman—Wonder Woman. Well, more specifically, Lynda Carter, the actress who played Wonder Woman in the 1970s TV show.

When he was little, he dreamed of guest-starring on the show and becoming friends with

Lynda. So when he won his lottery winnings, he knew *exactly* what he was going to do with his money. He would make his dream come true.

Mark hired a group of the world's most brilliant scientists (recommended to him by Triple J). Then he explained, "I want you to build me a time machine so I can go back in time to the 1970s."

"That is immoral!" one scientist said.

"It's dangerous!" said another.

"You could destroy the fabric of all space and time!" said a third.

Mark threw his money at them. All of it. Every dime. The scientists suddenly changed their tune.

"What a fantastic idea!" one scientist said.

"A brilliant use of money!" said another.

"Let's get started!" said a third.

So this group of scientists worked night and day for weeks until they had finally built a real-life time machine. "It'll only work *twice*," the scientists warned. "Once to go there, and once to come back. Got it?"

"Got it!" Mark said. He hopped inside and pushed the button. The whole world outside turned into bright light. The machine shook so hard, Mark thought his brains were going to poop out of his ears.

Instead, the time machine popped out on the set of *Wonder Woman*. "Who are you?" asked the director.

"I'm a time traveler from the future. I came back in time to see if I could be a guest star on the *Wonder Woman* TV show."

"Are you SAG?" the director asked.

"What's SAG?" Mark asked.

"Screen Actors Guild," the director said. "You can't be on TV unless you're part of the labor union."

Mark slapped himself in the face. He should have done a little more research before coming all the way back in time. He was so bummed. He

wandered toward his time machine, kicking rocks as he went.

"Why the frown, kid?" someone asked.

Mark turned around. "Lynda Carter?!"

"That's me." She smiled with her perfect smile.

Mark suddenly didn't care about being on TV anymore. He had finally met his big crush. He explained everything that had happened. And then he and Lynda had a good laugh about it. She even taught him to do her Wonder Woman spin. Afterward, she autographed a black-and-white picture for him. She signed it *To my favorite time traveler. Love, Lynda.*

When Mark came home, back to the present day, he didn't have any more money, but he was the happiest boy in Classroom 13.

CHAPTER 18
Mya & Madison

Mya & Madison felt *twice* as lucky as everyone else in Classroom 13. This was because they were twins.

These twins had two of everything—two matching beds, two matching toothbrushes, two matching unicycles, and, yes, two matching checks for $1,037,037,037.04.

Some of the kids wondered if the sisters would combine their lottery winnings for a whopping total of $2,074,074,074.08. That would make them *twice* as rich as everyone else.

But the twins didn't want to keep the money. They wanted to spend it.

As they almost always did, Mya & Madison had the exact same thought, at the exact same time: "We should each buy two of EVERY-THING and put it on a boat!" Mya & Madison said at the same time. "Like a Noah's Ark... *of stuff!*"

"But if we each buy *two* of the same thing, then we'll have *four* of everything—which is weird, because we're not quadruplets," Madison said.

"Ew. Quadruplets are weird," Mya said. "Well, if we each buy *one* of something, then together, we'll have *two* of everything!"

Mya & Madison smiled at the exact same time and said, "Then we'll have *twice* as much stuff as everybody else!"

The Ark of Stuff plan was a go.

Mya & Madison shopped until they dropped—

well, at least until their feet hurt. The girls went on a shopping spree, buying two of everything they'd ever wanted.

They bought two sequined pantsuits, two bedazzled cell phones, two glittered swimming pools, two emerald-crusted backpacks, two diamond-covered bicycles, two opal Hula-Hoops, two golden trampolines, and so on. (If there was anything shiny and expensive, they had two of it.)

Then, using their father's top secret military connections, the girls bought two aircraft carriers and had all their high-priced items flown there in helicopters.

The twins wanted to show off their spendings. So they planned a huge party on the ships and invited all their classmates from Classroom 13. Unfortunately, before the celebration, their ships were so heavy, they sank.

Because they were twins, Mya & Madison felt *twice* as sad about their loss.

CHAPTER 19
Dev

Dev's whole life revolved around video games. He'd go to sleep playing his PlayStation and move over to the Xbox when he woke up. On his way to school, he played his portable Nintendo. He also had over a hundred games on his phone for playing in between—and sometimes *during*—bathroom breaks.

"Are you pooping or playing video games in there?!" his dad would yell at the bathroom door.

"Both!" Dev answered.

So when Dev got his check for over a billion dollars, he knew what he wanted—to level up to *VIRTUAL REALITY*.

(His thumbs were getting tired of all the button mashing anyway.)

A store-bought VR system was *not* going to cut it for Dev. He wanted to live his life *inside* the most sophisticated virtual-reality world money could buy. So he found the greatest video game designers in the world and hired them.

"I want to *live* in a video game world," Dev said.

"For how long?" one game designer asked.

"*Forever,*" Dev said.

"But what about sleeping, or eating?" another game designer asked. "Or you know, going number one, or...you know, number two..."

"I'll be doing everything in this game world," Dev said. Then he handed his check over to the game designers. "Now get coding!"

The game designers worked twenty-four hours a day, seven days a week, to finish Dev's Virtual World in just one month. Many nights, they skipped sleeping to make Dev's deadline. To meet his demands, they skipped over some *tiny details*, but they could always add stuff later.

"Are you done yet?!" Dev snapped.

"Not quite," the designers said. "We need to add a Save function."

"Don't bother," Dev said. "I'm never leaving this game."

Dev stepped into the VR suit and turned on his new world. He couldn't believe his eyes.

The virtual reality was so crisp and so clear, it was like being in the real world—only way better because it wasn't real. In VR, Dev could fly like Superman. He could build castles with a wave of his virtual glove. He could fight monsters, drive race cars and rockets, and shoot up killer robots. He could even nap on a virtual cloud.

And when he had to use the restroom...well, he just went wherever. (The VR suit took care of the...*stuff*.)

Dev's VR was everything he could ever dream of and more. He ate virtual pizzas, rode virtual roller coasters, went on virtual quests, and met virtual friends from his favorite video games. In his game, there was no school and no chores and no nagging parents. And best of all, every day was an adventure.

Out of nowhere, Dev could kinda, sorta hear someone yelling (from back in the real world). He didn't want to deal with it, whatever it was. He wanted to play his game. With his glove, Dev turned up the volume. Now all he could hear was the cool techno music of his latest mission.

Suddenly, the virtual world around him vanished. There was nothing but black in every direction, until a blinking red light appeared overhead. Big capital letters appeared in the VR:

NO SAVE FILE FOUND. PROGRESS LOST.

Dev removed his VR goggles, returning to the *real* world. He was ready to shout at the VR game programmers. Instead, he screamed. He was surrounded by electrical sparks and a small fire.

FWWSSSSSHHHHHHH!

The programmers sprayed him (and the VR suit) down with fire extinguishers. "What happened?!" Dev cried.

"Sorry, little dude," one of the programmers said. "The system overheated and caught fire."

"But the game is okay, right?"

The VR programmers shook their head.

Dev sighed. It was officially *Game Over* for Dev's Virtual World. Now he was stuck in reality like the rest of the people on the planet.

CHAPTER 20
Ethan

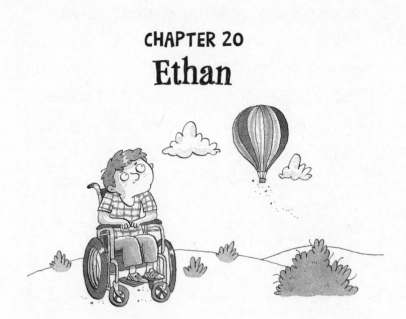

Ethan Earhart's parents were both lawyers. He hoped one day to grow up to be just like them. Ham or turkey? Paper or plastic? Boxers or briefs? Everything was something that could be argued. And he loved to argue.

"Six times nine is fifty-four," Ms. Linda said.

"Objection!" Ethan yelled.

"This is *not* a courtroom, Ethan. This is math.

Numbers don't lie. Six times nine *is* fifty-four."

"But how do we know that for sure? That numbers don't lie? Isn't a one lying about being an *odd* number? It does not look at all odd to me. In fact, it looks rather normal. One might say it looks fair, or *even*! But ten? Ten looks odd!"

"That's not how that works," Ms. Linda said.

"I disagree."

"That doesn't prove that numbers lie."

"I beg to differ."

Ethan was not doing this to be rude. Quite the contrary, Ethan was trying to be *judicious*— which meant showing good sense.

"No, it doesn't," Ethan said.

"Yes, it does," I (Honest Lee) said back.

"I beg to differ."

"Well, let's agree to disagree—hey, wait! Why are you debating with *me*?" I said. "*I'm* the narrator. Argue with your friends. I'm just a voice in this book!"

Anyway.

After Ethan found he had $1,037,037,037.04 to spend, his first idea was to buy a hot-air balloon. After all, he'd always wanted to fly in one. (Ethan was in a wheelchair, but he wouldn't let that stop him from seeing the world, or becoming the world's best lawyer.)

But as usual, Ethan began a list of pros and cons for buying a hot-air balloon.

Pros: Flight. Seeing the land from up high. Cool story.

Cons: Height. Falling to my death. Birds trying to steal my lunch.

Over the next few days, Ethan argued with himself. He was so stuck on this topic that he went back and forth and back and forth, arguing both sides of *buying* a hot-air balloon and *not buying* a hot-air balloon. He asked other students their thoughts.

"Buy a comic!" Fatima said.

"Buy a cat!" Emma said.

"Buy a fart!" Liam said.

"No, I don't want any of those," Ethan said. "Especially that last one."

After days without sleep, Ethan found himself yelling, "Objection!" at himself. Finally, he found one more pro than con. And that settled it.

He bought a hot-air balloon.

That weekend, Ethan withdrew the remaining $1,036,987,037.04 and loaded it into the balloon's passenger basket. Before boarding himself, he debated (with himself) about whether he should fly east or west first. And of course, that debate took a good, long while.

While Ethan argued with himself, the balloon broke away—with his money, but without him. A strong gust of wind caught the balloon and blew it up into the air.

"Hey, that's my balloon!" Ethan yelled. (But then argued with himself, "Is it, though, or does the balloon own itself?")

Ethan watched as his hot-air balloon—and his fortune—disappeared into the clouds.

The balloon made global headlines the next day. Apparently, every time the wind blew, the sky rained money. All over the world, people watched for the money balloon, calling it "a wonderful, beautiful miracle."

Ethan begged to differ.

CHAPTER 21
Chloe

Is there a canned good in your house that you don't know what to do with? Do you know someone who likes meals delivered to their home? Perhaps you want to save the dolphins, but don't know where to start?

Well, just ask Chloe. Chloe cares. About *everything*.

Chloe Canter never met a cause she didn't

want to take up. She organized four blood drives and twelve fund-raisers last year. She raised awareness about deforestation by chaining herself to a tree. When Classroom 13 needed a new water bottle for the class hamster, she hosted a telethon.

(She raised over six hundred dollars. For a tiny bottle. For a hamster.)

That's *how much* Chloe cares.

Naturally, Chloe already knew where her lottery money was going when Ms. Linda wrote her a check. Her winnings were going straight to CHARITY.

But how would she divide up the money? There were so many charities that needed her help: The one that gave free diapers to single moms. The one that built schools in poor countries. The one that set aside land for lions. Even the one that taught street kids how to steal nicer clothes. (That is a charity, isn't it?)

"You should give it all to one charity," Ava said. "That would make a big difference."

"You should give a little bit to every charity that exists," Teo said. "That will make lots of little differences."

"You should just fart on it," Liam blurted, making a loud fart noise.

Chloe ignored Liam. She considered Ava's and Teo's suggestions. She finally decided she wanted to make a big difference. But which charity would she select?

Chloe thought hard. The lottery winnings came to her at random. So that was how she should donate the money.

Chloe went online and found a list of every major charity on the planet. There were over 1.5 million charities in the United States alone. So she closed her eyes, scrolled down through the webpage, and let her mouse land on a random charity.

She opened her eyes. "National Flatulence

Awareness, a nonprofit," she read. "What's *flatulence?*"

Liam's eyes grew wide. "It means *fart!*"

Chloe thought Liam was kidding, so she looked it up. "Flatulence" did, in fact, mean intestinal gas, which is what a fart is.

Chloe shrugged. If fate wanted her to use her winnings to make America more aware of farts, then that's what she had to do. *Farts have feelings, too,* she thought.

She phoned the Flatulence Awareness hotline and made her donation. The woman on the other end of the phone nearly fainted. "Thank you! Bless you, my child!" Chloe heard the woman pass gas on the other end of the phone. "I apologize. I expel gas when I am excited."

That night, Chloe felt good. She had made a real difference in the world. She was warming up to the idea of educating people through National Flatulence Awareness, when a public service announcement on TV came on. An oil tanker crashed off the coast of a place called Penguin Cove. Oil was everywhere.

A single tear leaked out from behind Chloe's glasses and down her cheek.

"Oh no!" she said, running to the phone. She called the Flatulence Awareness hotline. "Earlier today, I donated over a billion dollars, and I'm afraid I made a mistake. I need the money back— not for me, of course. But for the oil-coated penguins! You know, for a *real* charity."

After a long *pooooooooot*, the woman said, "Pardon me. I expel gas when I am offended."

"Why are you offended?" Chloe asked.

"Because your change of heart really *stinks*."

Chloe didn't know how to respond to that.

"Ah, I see," the woman said. "The silent but deadly treatment. Well, the money is gone. And there's nothing that can be done. She who dealt it...well, you know how the rest goes. Good day, ma'am."

CHAPTER 22
Fatima

All the kids in Classroom 13 knew one thing about Fatima: She had "issues."

No, not *someone-call-the-cops-on-that-girl* kind of "issues." I mean, actual *issues*...of comic books. Fatima Farooq was a comic book collector with a rather serious collection. She bought two of every comic: one to read and a second that remained—perfectly safe and in mint

condition—in a plastic slipcover, inside a protective box, never to be touched by human hands.

I bet you can guess what she bought with her share of the lottery winnings.

(What? Who said a refrigerator? Yes, you did. I heard you. Now stop talking back to this book or people are going to think *you* have "issues.")

Fatima used her lottery winnings to buy every comic book ever made. Even the super-rare ones owned by pale old men who swore they'd never part with their most-prized possessions.

She bought *classic* issues, *deluxe* issues, *autographed* issues, *misprinted* issues, and issues with *die-cut holographic foil*. She bought superhero comics, ninja comics, monster comics, robot comics, sci-fi comics, and old cartoon comic strips that were hanging up in a comic book museum in another state.

Fatima bought them all, spending every last cent.

Her mother did *not* approve.

"Fatima Farooq!" her mom yelled from deep within the stacks and stacks of comic books that now lined every square inch of their house. "What is all this?!"

"My comic book collection!" she yelled back. "It's finally complete."

With all the stacks of comics and mountains of boxes and layers of protective plastic everywhere, it took Mrs. Farooq six grueling days to dig a tunnel to her daughter's bedroom. Mrs. Farooq wore full climbing gear, including a little helmet with a light on it. Her face was covered in brightly colored stains (from smudging the pages along the way), and her hands were shaking.

"What have I told you about comic books?" Mrs. Farooq growled.

"But, Mom—" Fatima said. "I have some educational comics, too! Look," she pleaded, pulling out an issue to show. "This guy *learned* how to melt minds with a mind-melting laser! Knowledge *is* power!"

Mrs. Farooq was not amused. "What have I told you...?"

Fatima repeated her mother's words. "Comics are bad news..."

"And..."

"And young, vulnerable minds shouldn't be reading them," Fatima and her mom said together.

Mrs. Farooq took out her phone and started dialing.

The next morning, a fleet of garbage trucks rolled up to Fatima's house. Soon, her billion-dollar comic collection—the biggest one in the world, I'm told—would fill landfills across the country. And birds would poop on it.

Honest Lee does NOT agree with Mrs. Farooq. Comics are NOT bad news. They are GREAT, and everyone should read them.

CHAPTER 23
Yuna

Ask anyone: Yuna is a *mystery*.

Much to the annoyance of her classmates—and Ms. Linda—Yuna speaks only in code. Instead of words, Yuna uses numbers to communicate. The numbers correspond to each letter in the alphabet. Meaning:

A = 1

B = 2

C = 3

D = 4

E = 5

And so on...counting upward until you reach the letter Z, which of course equals 26.

What's that? You want to know what Yuna did with her money? Well, all I'm going to say is what she told me:

25-21-14-1 8-9-4 8-5-18
13-15-14-5-25 19-15-13-5-23-8-5-18-5
19-5-3-18-5-20.
19-15 19-5-3-18-5-20, 19-8-5
6-15-18-7-15-20 23-8-5-18-5 9-20 23-1-19.

CHAPTER 24
Benji

Benji had very BIG—or should I say, very *small*—plans for his new fortune.

"I'm going to *shrink* them all!" he told his parents. Benji was smiling ear to ear. His mom and dad were nervous, until they realized he wasn't talking about shrinking every *person* in the world.

He was talking about shrinking their *pets*.

You see, Benji had two loves: football and

animals. He loved animals, but he loved *miniature* animals even more: Panda cows and micro pigs. Bee hummingbirds and Philippine tarsiers. And let's not forget miniature horses and teensy-weensy fennec foxes. (I blame the Internet, and all its videos of tiny, itty-bitty animals that are cuter than cute.)

Benji had a stuffed animal collection (on the same shelf as his football trophies), but it just wasn't the same. He wanted real-life mini pets. He wanted to hold them and hug them and love them and live happily ever after.

Have you ever seen a pygmy marmoset? (Look it up.) It's no bigger than the palm of your hand. It could live in your shirt pocket. Benji wanted one. And he wanted everyone to have one. Everyone deserved a little bit of miniature joy.

"Think about it," Benji told his parents. "If everyone had a teacup puppy to carry around all day, no one would be sad. You can't be sad when you look at that tiny, furry cuteness with its big, beautiful eyes. Plus, they're perfect for football practice—you can pull them out and cuddle with them in between plays."

Benji's parents didn't understand their son.

Triple J and Mark recommended the same scientists who helped them. "They *really* like money. Like, way *more* than they like obeying the laws of nature and space-time and whatnot. If you're willing to pay, they'll pretty much do whatever you want."

So Benji hired the scientists to build him a *shrink ray*. It looked like a huge laser cannon from an old sci-fi movie. Once charged, it shot a beam that could miniaturize *anything*.

"Big, scary animals become tiny, cutesy animals," said one scientist.

"Extra cutesy!" another scientist added, counting his money.

"How can I be sure it works?" Benji asked.

Just then, a shrunken scientist the size of an action figure climbed onto his shoulder. "Trust me," his wee voice squeaked, "*it works*."

Benji was so excited to get started, he bought two local pet stores, a farm, and the nearest zoo.

One by one, Benji put the animals in front of the shrink ray. He pulled the lever and watched them shrink down to the size of an apple. He could hardly believe it—petting and holding each of the impossibly tiny animals made him smile so hard, it hurt. (But in a good way.)

With each new animal, he knocked another wish off his wish list. Pygmy marmosets in his shirt pocket? Check. Walking a miniature horse on a leash? Done-zo. Teacup puppies nestled safely in his gym bag for halftime cuddles? Mission accomplished.

Benji invited Classroom 13 to his miniature zoo. He reminded everyone, "Be careful where you step!"

His fellow students lost their minds. Everyone wanted one. And Benji wanted everyone to be able to have the same kind of strange love that he had. So he planned to open his zoo to the public and give one animal away to anyone who wanted one. Unfortunately, before he could start giving away his tiny animals (and help the world to find love and happiness), several things happened all at once:

1. The local pet stores got together and sued Benji for making impossibly cute animals. They couldn't compete with that. Local law enforcement took away Benji's shrink ray until the trial was settled.

2. PETA (People for the Ethical Treatment of Animals) protested his new zoo and his giving away animals to anyone who wanted them. They thought everyone should be screened. Their lawyers also sued Benji. His zoo was closed to the public until the trial was settled.

3. His parents sat him down when he came

home. They also had their lawyers with them. "You've shrunk enough things for now," his mom's lawyer said. "Time to *grow* your bank account."

"Your parents put the rest of your money in a savings account," the lawyers said. "That way, it can collect interest."

"But what about helping the world find love through miniature pets? It could bring world peace!"

"Your dreams will have to wait until you're older," his mom's lawyer said.

"When?" he asked.

"When you're eighteen," the lawyers said.

Benji was upset that he couldn't help the rest of the world find miniature happiness. But for now, at least, Benji was happy. When the cops and lawyers weren't looking, Benji managed to sneak a handful of plum-sized pets into his pockets....

CHAPTER 25
Preeya

Preeya is best friends with Olivia Ogilvy. (You know, the girl who put all her money in the bank for college instead of having fun with it.)

Sorry. I mean: Preeya *was* best friends with Olivia. (Past tense.)

Why aren't they best friends anymore? Well, Preeya's mom is friends with Olivia's mom, and you know how moms like to share *everything*.

At their weekly poker night, Olivia's mom said, "Oh goodness. I am so proud of Olivia for putting all her lottery money away for college."

That night, Preeya's mom went straight home and said, "Preeya, give me your lottery check. We're going straight to the bank to deposit it into your college fund—just like Olivia did."

Preeya was *not* happy. She didn't want to save her money for college. She wanted to spend it *now*. She planned to use her money to become famous so that she could win the heart of a certain famous male pop star—you know the one: super cute, super talented, sings love songs that make your heart swell (even though you tell everyone you *don't* like his music, even though secretly you *do*).

Preeya was furious.

But maybe—hopefully—she'll be more appreciative when she's older.

(I doubt it.)

CHAPTER 26
Liam

The students of Classroom 13 have always wondered: How is it that *little* Liam is able to make such *big* farts?

Liam's gas ranged from silent-but-deadly to trombone-loud-but-without-a-smell. It was quite the talent.

Mason guessed he ate chili for breakfast, lunch, and dinner. Triple J guessed he trained with an order of butt-blasting monks in Tibet.

Ximena guessed he was simply born with a gift for gas.

The truth was...*practice*. After all, practice makes perfect. And Liam, the class prankster, worked very hard to create controlled farts, which he used for comedic effect. His favorite phrase was: "Pull my finger."

If he tells you to do this—trust me—*don't*.

Liam tried to get laughs to distract others from how *small* and *short* he was. He did not like being the smallest student in Classroom 13. He dreamed *big*. In fact, he's always dreamed of being in the *Global Book of World Records*.

So when he won the lottery, he decided to spend his $1,037,037,037.04 on making his dreams come true. How? Well, he liked pranking people, but that was no way to get a world record. But he did like eating. (No matter how much he ate, he never gained weight thanks to a very fast metabolism.)

Finally, he decided on a worthy world record— Most Desserts Ever Eaten by a Human Being.

Liam planned on spending his fortune devouring every kind of sweet treat imaginable and going down in history for it.

Liam phoned the Global World Record office and informed them of his plan. They sent two representatives to join Liam on his world travels. Dan and Dana would follow Liam with a camera and a journal to document his progress.

The journey began in Switzerland, home to the world's finest chocolatiers. Liam sampled thousands of varieties of chocolate in one sitting and washed it all down with molten liquid cocoa from a chocolate fountain.

Dan and Dana gave a thumbs-up and said, "Good start."

In Russia, Liam ate truckloads of Kiev cake. In South Africa, he spooned malva pudding down his throat. In Brazil, he consumed tres leches cakes. In Belgium, Liam devoured chocolate chip waffles. He licked up liquid nitrogen ice cream in Manila and ais kacang in Malaysia.

In Australia, he forked in lamingtons. In Japan, he inhaled trays of green tea mochi. In Turkey, Liam swallowed pans of baklava. In Hawaii, he ate haupia delights until he couldn't take another bite. He ate deep-fried candy bars in Scotland and then chocolate-covered chapulines in Mexico. (You should probably *not* look up what *chapulines* are....)

(I told you not *to look them up.)*

Finally, Liam went to Paris to eat the world's most expensive dessert: a seventy-seven-scoop sundae covered in gold dust and real diamonds. Once he finished, he would be a Global World Record holder.

He began to shovel the dessert down his throat. Four spoonfuls from finishing, Liam got light-headed and his stomach began to rumble. "Can I have some water?" he asked Dan and Dana. "I'm not feeling so—"

Liam keeled over and *died*.

It's okay. It was only for a few seconds.

Dan and Dana were not just judges. They were also certified paramedics. They zapped Liam with heart paddles. Twenty thousand volts of electricity surged through Liam's veins—along with massive amounts of sugar and dairy.

As Liam came back to life, he let out the loudest, most powerful, earth-rumbling fart a human body had ever produced. The entire restaurant shook.

As the Global World Record reps helped him to sit up, Liam said, "I think I'm done with sweets."

Liam did *not* break the record for Most Desserts Ever Eaten by a Human Being. But he *did* break the record for Most Powerful Fart Ever Farted by a Human Being.

Dan and Dana noted: "The shock wave of the fart was felt as far away as Spain. It was seismic!"

Liam could live with that.

CHAPTER 27
Isabella

Isabella Inglebel loved horses.

To no one's surprise, Isabella bought herself the biggest horse ranch in America. How many horses can $1,037,037,037.04 buy you?

Well, it depends on the age, health, fame, and breed of the horse. But all in all, Isabella bought exactly 312,462 horses.

Now Isabella Inglebel owns 312,462 horses.

Or, I should say, *owned* 312,462 horses. (Past tense.)

You see, Isabella's hired horseman—an old cowboy named Old Blue—told her she needed a fence for her horses. But Isabella didn't want her beloved pets to feel fenced in. She wanted them to run free.

And they ran free all right.

All those wild horses galloped off into the sunset, never to return. No amount of carrots or apples or hay could lure them back. Isabella should have listened to Old Blue.

CHAPTER 28
Hugo

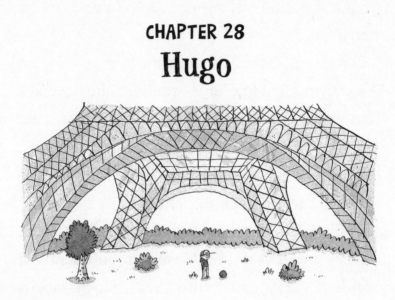

Hugo Houde est né et a grandi à Paris. Quand Hugo avait dix ans, sa famille a dû partir vivre à l'étranger pour le travail de son père. C'est ainsi qu'Hugo a atterri dans la classe numéro treize où personne ne parlait français.

La France lui manquait énormément. Comme il ne pouvait pas y retourner, il décida d'amener la France à lui. Alors, avec son argent, il acheta la tour Eiffel et la mit dans son jardin. C'est la vie.

CHAPTER 29
Zoey

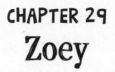

Unlike her classmates, Zoey was not in a hurry to spend her winnings. She was already rich, so all she wanted to do was cash the check and bring all the money back to her house. She wanted to be surrounded by the cash.

So Zoey did just that.

An entire fleet of armored cars full of cash followed her home from the bank. When they pulled into her driveway, the guards asked,

"Where do you want this?"

Zoey hadn't thought about it. Then she remembered seeing a cartoon about a greedy duck. He had so much money, he could jump off a diving board and swim around in it, like a swimming pool.

Zoey liked that. She wouldn't have to spend the money, but it wouldn't just be sitting around gathering dust either.

"In the backyard," Zoey said. "Put the money in the pool!"

The guards unzipped the bags and dumped the stacks of cash into her swimming pool—right into the water.

"You're going to ruin that money," her dad said.

Zoey ignored him.

Her dad shrugged and let Zoey do as she wanted. After all, it was *her* money.

She ran inside to put on her bathing suit and swim goggles.

Once Zoey's entire fortune was in the pool, she somersaulted off her trampoline and into the pool of money.

Ker-splash—CRASH!

With so much soggy paper, the water didn't feel very good when she dove in. In fact, it felt like diving into the shallow end of a pool. Zoey knocked up her elbows and knees rather badly.

She didn't care, though. She wanted to swim in money. But swimming through the cash-filled water was like swimming through oatmeal. If that weren't bad enough, all the dollar bills made it tough to see underwater. Zoey swam right into the pool's wall and bumped her head.

After a few minutes, she noticed that her red hair was turning green. But worse, the cash was dissolving into mush. Her fortune was melting.

"Dad! Dad! What's happening to my money?!" she screamed.

"I told you it would ruin the money," her dad said. "This morning, the pool man treated the water with special cleaning chemicals—chemicals strong enough to destroy the leaves at the bottom of the pool."

Or anything else paper thin for that matter, I should add.

Zoey leaped out of the pool and watched her fortune disintegrate into green soup. She stormed inside, upset and penniless.

She cried as she took a bubble bath—in regular, plain old water—just like normal (poor) people.

CHAPTER 30

Really Unlucky Ms. Linda

Lucky Ms. Linda's luck was about to change. (Again.)

Ms. Linda was having a wonderful day. She'd had a very pricey brunch ($2,000 for scrambled eggs and toast). Her anti-bird shampoo made her hair shine and bounce like a supermodel's ($20,000 a bottle). And she was about to buy her dream house—the most expensive estate in the state ($200,000,000).

"All you have to do is sign here," the real estate agent said, "and the mansion will be yours."

Ms. Linda looked at the sky to see if there were any thunderclouds. (There weren't.) It was a beautiful and sunny day. She breathed a sigh of relief. She signed the contract and shook the real estate agent's hand.

"Congratulations on your new home!" he said.

Ms. Linda stepped into her beautiful dream house and squealed a happy squeal. She was unaware of a slight rumble beneath her.

Ms. Linda spent every last dime of her fortune to make the house *perfect*. She hired Emma's parents (the "interior decorators") to tell her exactly what furniture to buy. They helped her order rugs from countries she could not pronounce and purchase silverware from the fanciest stores in New York City. She even purchased the famous *Mona Lisa* painting by Da Vinci and hung it in her living room.

The house was everything Ms. Linda had dreamed of and more...

...which is why Ms. Linda tried to ignore the odd things. For example, no matter how many times she got them fixed, her floors remained uneven. The countertops were also not right. If she put a plate on the counter, the dish would slide off and shatter onto the floor.

She called the real estate agent. He said, "Oh, that. It's just the house settling."

One day, Ms. Linda nearly broke her leg, falling into the driveway. It seemed her front porch had risen six feet above the sidewalk. This made getting in and out of her house a real challenge.

She called the real estate agent. He said, "Oh, that. Watch your step."

When she tried to host a dinner party for some of the other teachers, her house began to creak and shake. It was so noticeable that her friends asked, "Is it haunted?"

"No, no," Ms. Linda said. "My house just has a lot of personality."

One sunny day, Ms. Linda decided on a quiet game of croquet in her front yard. She raised the mallet and hit the ball. When the ball struck her house, the ground caved in and swallowed her house whole.

Ms. Linda peered into the pit in the ground. She saw her fancy furniture and beautiful dishes and the *Mona Lisa*—all destroyed. Her dream home had been swallowed up by a *sinkhole*.

Good thing Ms. Linda was smart enough to get insurance.

"I'm sorry, ma'am," said the insurance adjuster. "The sinkhole that destroyed your home is *not* covered by your insurance."

Several birds dove at Ms. Linda to pull at her hair. She tried to swat them away but quickly gave up.

⭐   ⭐   ⭐

Everything in Classroom 13 returned to the way it was before Ms. Linda won the lottery. Life was normal again. Well, as *normal* as Classroom 13 gets.

Ms. Linda was still late to class, Santiago was still sick, Hugo was still French, and Earl was still a hamster. Triple J may or may not have had clones running around. Yuna still didn't know where her fortune was. And Mason's best friend was still a crossing guard that gave him fresh milk every morning.

The truth be told: Winning lots of money—and losing lots of money—hadn't changed anyone's lives all that much.

In fact, no one in Classroom 13 had really learned *anything*.

What a shame.

Did you learn anything?

No? I didn't think you would. Honestly.

CHAPTER 31
Your Chapter

That's right—it's your turn!

Grab some paper and a writing utensil. (Not a fork, silly. Try a pencil or pen.) Or if you have one of those fancy computer doo-hickeys, use that. Now tell me...

If you won the lottery what would *YOU* do with the money?!

When you're done, share it with your teacher, your family, and your friends. (Don't forget your pets! Pets like to hear stories, too.) You can even ask your parents to send me your chapter at the address below.

HONEST LEE

LITTLE, BROWN BOOKS FOR YOUNG READERS

1290 Avenue of the Americas

New York, NY 10104